# Amanda's Big Dream

written by Judith Matz

illustrated by Elizabeth Patch

# Amanda's Big Dream
written by Judith Matz, LCSW
illustrated by Elizabeth Patch

## A Note to Adults:

Children express concerns about body size at younger ages than ever before,
and adults are getting all kinds of messages about kids and weight.
Amanda's Big Dream offers a fun way to start important and positive conversations.

We ask adults to keep in mind that your own attitudes toward weight affect children.
While a thinner body is typically valued in our culture, people naturally come in all shapes and sizes.

Unfortunately, when the focus is placed on weight, rather than on healthful behaviors,
kids who are bigger often experience shame and kids who are smaller often fear becoming fat.
Eating disorders, low self-esteem, and weight bullying are some of the harmful consequences
that come from an emphasis on having a thinner body.

Let's teach kids to respect their bodies and those of others.
Let's model positive behaviors that help them become healthy, strong and confident.
Let's help create a world where everyone can follow their dreams!

## Visit amandasbigdream.com

- Resources for Parents, Teachers and Other Caregivers
- Amanda's Big Dream Conversation Guide by Judith Matz, LCSW
- Printable coloring pages by illustrator Elizabeth Patch.

**Graceful Cat Press**
ISBN-13: 978-0-692-37781-9
ISBN-10: 0692377816
BISAC: Juvenile Fiction / Concepts / Body

To you, dear reader:
May you follow your dreams
and let your heart soar!
Judith Matz

To my mother, Adrienne Gloria Patch,
who put the very first crayon in my hands.
Elizabeth Patch

Amanda dreamed of getting a solo in the Spring Ice Show.

"Do you think I'll make it?" Amanda asked her mother.

"I believe in you Amanda," she said with a smile.

"Remember what we always say..."

"I know, Mom," Amanda interrupted.

"Follow your dreams, whoever you are.
  Follow your dreams and they'll take you far."

At practice on Tuesday, Amanda laced up her shiny pink skates and slid onto the ice. Her heart beat with excitement as she warmed up for her lesson.

"Your skating is coming along beautifully," Coach Sarah said, clapping her hands.
"Keep up the good work! And remember to practice, practice, practice!"
"I will, Coach Sarah. I really want to get a solo," Amanda replied.

"Well, Amanda, you're one of our strongest skaters.
But I wonder if you could get even closer to the ice on your sit spin
if you lost a little weight. That might help your chances."

Amanda felt like a sparkling bubble that had just been burst.
No one had ever said anything about her weight before.
What if she couldn't get a solo even though she was trying so hard?

As soon as she saw her mom, Amanda burst into tears.

"What's the matter, Amanda?"

Amanda didn't say anything at first.

Then she whispered the words that Coach Sarah said to her.

Amanda tried to make Coach Sarah's words go away,
but they kept ringing in her ears.
What could she do?
She knew she was bigger than some of her friends,
but that had never stopped her from anything before.

At dinner that night, Amanda blurted,
"I don't think I'll get a solo unless I lose weight."
"That's not true, Amanda," her mother said. "I believe in you."
"You're fine just the way you are, Amanda," said her father.
"The important thing is to try."

"I know," Amanda chimed in as she sat up straighter.
"Follow your dreams, whoever you are.
 Follow your dreams and they'll take you far!"
"But what if Coach Sarah is right?" Amanda mumbled.
"Why don't we check in with Dr. Jones?" her mom asked gently.

"It's so nice to see you, Amanda. What can I do for you today?"
Amanda told Dr. Jones about her dream of having a solo
and what Coach Sarah said.
"I know you get lots of good exercise with your skating, Amanda,
so your body is physically fit. That's great," said Dr. Jones.
Amanda grinned.

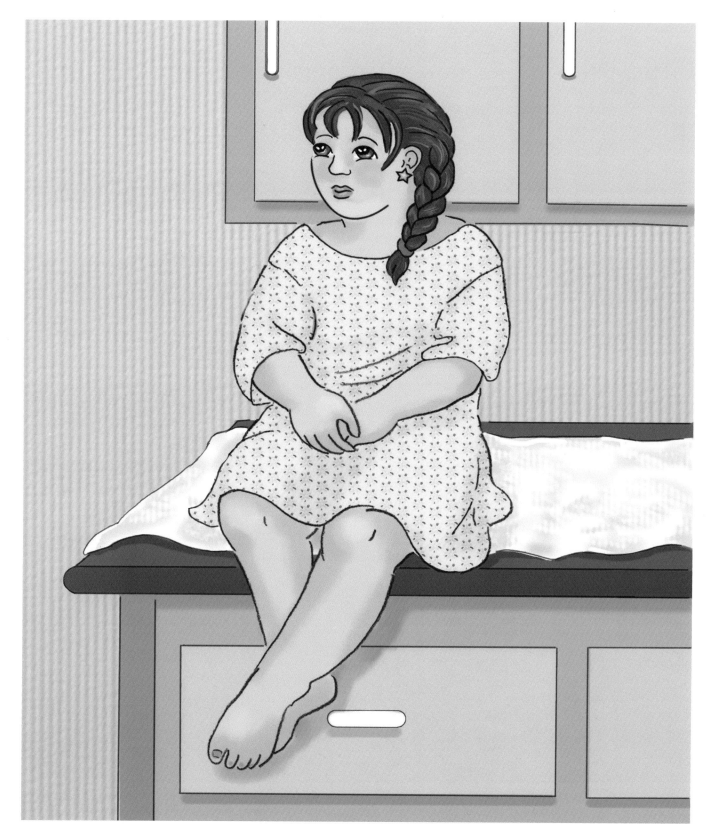

"Your mom tells me you get plenty of sleep too, and have lots of energy.
I know you also do a good job of listening to your stomach to tell you when
you're hungry. You choose a wide variety of foods that satisfy you,
and stop eating when you are full."
Amanda nodded.

Dr. Jones listened to Amanda's heart and checked her ears, nose, and throat. "I'm happy to tell you that you're a very healthy girl. A lot of people think you can just decide how much you want to weigh, but that's not true. Bodies come in all shapes and sizes, Amanda. The most important thing is to keep making choices that are healthy for your body. That's how we'll know your body is exactly the right weight for you." Amanda smiled.

The next day Amanda raced to put on her shiny pink skates. She stuck her leg out behind her in a fast turning camel spin, and without missing a beat lowered herself into a sit spin. But she couldn't get any closer to the ice than before. Amanda's thoughts started spinning too.

What if Coach Sarah was right and Dr. Jones was wrong?

Was she really too big to get a solo in the Spring Ice Show?

Amanda noticed her best friend Christine was landing a new jump.
"Maybe if I learn to do an axel too,
I'll have a better chance of getting a solo," she thought.
Coach Sarah showed Amanda how to push off her skate
so that she could learn to twirl in the air.
"But it will take practice, practice, practice," she reminded Amanda.

Amanda worked on her axel day after day, but no matter what she did,
her body just couldn't seem to make it all the way around.
She decided to give it one last shot.
Amanda gathered her speed, pushed off the ice,
and then KABOOM!

Amanda stood up and brushed off the ice.

"Are you okay, Amanda?" asked Christine.

"No!" said Amanda. "I'm just too fat and that's why I can't land my jump.
I'll never get a solo in the ice show." Christine put her arm around her friend.

"You know," she said, "I've been working on this jump for almost a year now.
You can't expect to get it right away."

Just then, Emily and Billy skated past her,
pointing and giggling as they whispered to each other.
Amanda was sure they must be talking about her weight.

"Ignore them," Christine said.
"Let's keep skating."

But Amanda couldn't stop worrying.
She wanted a solo more than anything in the world.
Was she too big? It just wasn't fair!
Without saying goodbye to Christine,
Amanda flew off the ice and went straight to the locker room.

Amanda unlaced her pink skates and threw them on the locker room floor.
If she couldn't have a solo, she didn't want to skate.

"I've been looking all over for you," Amanda's mom said
as she rushed into the locker room.
"I quit," shouted Amanda. "I'm not skating anymore."
"But the ice show..." continued her mother.
"NO! I'm done skating."

The next week, Amanda refused to go to her lessons.
She stopped practicing her leaps and jumps on the ice.
She stopped lacing up her pink skates.
But she couldn't stop dreaming.

One night Amanda pretended that she was the star of the ice show.
She put on her favorite outfit and leaped around her room.

Just as she twirled in the air, the door opened and her parents started clapping.
"Bravo!" they cried.
"I miss skating," Amanda murmured.

"Amanda, what do you see in that mirror?" asked her dad.

"I see me."

"Look more carefully. What else do you see in the mirror?"
Amanda stared at her reflection.

"I know," she exclaimed, "I see a skater!"

"That's right," said her mom. "You are a skater, Amanda!
And you remember what we always say..."
"I know, Mom," Amanda interrupted. "Follow your dreams, whoever you are.
Follow your dreams and they'll take you far!" And then Amanda knew:
The only way to make her big dream come true was to believe in herself.
And, of course, to practice, practice, practice!

The next day Amanda laced up her pink skates and rushed to the ice
so she could warm up for her lesson with Coach Sarah.
She wanted to be the best skater she could be!
As Amanda twirled and leaped on the ice,
she knew that whether or not she got a solo,
her dreams would always take her far.